1 3 5 7 9 10 8 6 4 2

Printed in China by WKT Company Limited, New Territories, Hong Kong
First American edition—2014
First published in hardcover in 2013 in the United Kingdom by Picadilly Press

Henry Holt books may be purchased for business or promotional use. For information
on bulk purchases, please contact Macmillan Corporate and Premium Sales Department
at (800) 221-7945 x5442 or by e-mail at specialmarkets@macmillan.com.

ISBN 978-0-8050-9918-8

Library of Congress Cataloging-in-Publication Data is available.

mackids.com
New York, New York 10010
175 Fifth Avenue
Publishers since 1866
Henry Holt and Company, LLC

For my little Junoberry

MY HUMONGOUS HAMSTER

Lorna Freytag

Henry Holt and Company
New York

My hamster doesn't do much.
He just sleeps and eats
and eats and sleeps.

Sometimes he gets so
HUNGRY
that I think he might eat his whole
bowl of food in one huge gulp.

If he does that, he will get
BIGGER and **BIGGER**.

Then he will be...

...HUMONGOUS!

He wouldn't fit into his cage
anymore, or my bedroom.
He would have to go outside.

He'd eat trees like broccoli.

He'd be a danger crossing the road.

But he'd have a lot of fun at the fair.

And he'd be able to see for

MILES!

He could give me and my

friends a ride to the park.

He might even help the police catch **CRIMINALS**.

He might rescue someone in trouble.

But he would also be
SCARY.

The cat wouldn't like him...

...nor would the neighbor's dog!

In fact, I think I'd find
him scary myself,

especially if he got **ANGRY.**

Would he sleep under a bridge,

in a circus tent,

at the foot of a mountain,

or in a barn?

I'm sure he'd miss us playing together.

So I think he would be
glad to shrink back to
normal hamster size again,

and be ready for
another hamster sleep,
in his usual hamster house...

...until the next time

he gets

HUMONGOUSLY

HUNGRY!